DINO-MIKE

AND THE
T. REX ATTACK!

WRITTEN & ILLUSTRATED BY FRANCO

STONE ARCH BOOKS
a capstone imprint

Dino-Mike! is published by
Stone Arch Books,
a Capstone imprint
1710 Roe Crest Drive
North Mankato, Minnesota 56003
www.capstonepub.com

Cataloging-in-Publication Data is available on
the Library of Congress website.

ISBN: 978-1-4342-9627-6 (library hardcover)
ISBN: 978-1-4342-9631-3 (paperback)
ISBN: 978-1-4965-0165-3 (eBook)

Summary: Dino-Mike is on the trail of a T. rex in
this chapter book adventure!

Printed in Canada.
092014   008478FRS15

CONTENTS

Young Mike Evans travels the world with
his dino-hunting dad. From the Jurassic
Coast in Great Britain to the Liaoning
Province in China, young Dino-Mike has been
there, *dug* that!

When his dad is dusting fossils, Mike's
boning up on his own dino skills — only he's
finding the real deal. A live T. rex egg! A
portal to the Jurassic Period!! An undersea
dinosaur sanctuary!!!

Prepare yourself for another wild and
wacky Dino-Mike adventure, which nobody
will *ever* believe . . .

Chapter 1
ROAR!

Inside a small tent, Mike Evans rested on a sleeping bag. A lantern flickered next to him. Outside, frogs croaked in the cool spring night.

Suddenly, a large shadow appeared on the wall of the tent. A T. rex!

"ROOOAAR!!" growled a voice.

"Ack!" Mike screamed, sitting up.

"Haha!" laughed Mike's dad, Stanley. He was twisting his hands in front of the lantern's light. "Not bad for a shadow puppet, huh, kiddo?"

"Very funny, Dad," said Mike, settling back into his sleeping bag. "Now I'll never sleep."

"You better rest up, son," his dad told him. "Tomorrow, maybe we'll dig up a *real* Tyrannosaurus rex."

"Really?!" Mike asked, excited.

"If we're lucky," his dad replied. He turned off the lantern. "Did you know the first T. rex fossils were found —?"

"Right here in Montana in 1902," Mike interrupted.

"Wow!" his dad exclaimed. "You sure know your dino facts! But did you know the T. rex is a theropod, meaning —?"

"It walked on two legs instead of four." Mike laughed. "You asked me that question last week, remember, Dad?"

"Now I do, but I almost forgot something else too," said his dad. He reached into his backpack and pulled out a present. "Since this is your first archeological dig, I got you something."

"Thanks, Dad!" Mike ripped into the present like a hungry dinosaur.

He pulled a shiny green sweatshirt out of the box. "Clothes?" he asked, disappointed.

"This is *special* jacket, Mike. A scientist friend of mine developed it," explained his dad. He ran his fingers over the fabric. "These scales look and act like the ones on a real dinosaur."

Mike gasped. "Whoa! Really?"

"Yep," his dad replied. "Try it on."

Mike scrambled out of his sleeping bag and put on the jacket. "It's perfect!" he exclaimed.

"That's not all," said his dad. He reached over Mike's shoulder and pulled the hood onto his head. "It's a hoodie!"

Mike's dad held up a mirror. The hood looked just like the head of a T. rex! A row of razor-sharp teeth lined the fringe. Two large yellow eyes glowed on either side of the hood.

Mike's dad clicked a button on the jacket's sleeve. **Beep! Beep!** The T. rex eyes lit up like headlights.

"Wow!" shouted Mike.

His dad clicked another button. **Pop! Pop! Pop!** Three diamond shapes burst from the back of the jacket.

"Are those —?" Mike began.

"Yep," his dad answered before his son could finish. "Stegosaurus plates! Actually, they're solar panels to power the jacket. They'll also keep the jacket nice and toasty warm."

Mike hugged his dad. "This is the best present ever!"

"I'm glad you like it, son," said his dad, "and I'm glad you're here with me." He slipped back into his sleeping bag. "Now let's get some shut-eye, kiddo. We have a big day of dinosaur digging tomorrow."

"You got it, Dad," Mike replied.

Mike lay down, pulled his sleeping bag up to his neck, and let his head sink into the pillow. He smiled.

Mike couldn't wait for the adventure to begin!

Chapter 2
T. REX!

"It's a T. rex!" shouted Mike's dad.

Other paleontologists ran to his side. The scientists carried shovels, pick axes, and brushes. They all stared at a giant bone sticking out of the dirt.

"Good find, Dad," said Mike. Wearing his new Dino Jacket, he squeezed in between the scientists for a closer look.

Mike zipped up his jacket and shook off the morning chill. The sun had barely risen, and the team had already been digging for hours.

"Does finding fossils always take this long?" Mike asked his dad.

"It sure does," his dad replied. He used a small brush to remove tiny bits of dirt from the T. rex bone. "We don't want the fossils to break!"

Mike kicked a few rocks on the ground and sighed.

"Tell you what," added his dad. "Why don't you go explore the other dig sites."

"Can I?" asked Mike excitedly.

"Of course," replied his dad, "but be back before dark, okay? We have the big Dinosaur BBQ tonight."

"I wouldn't miss it!" said Mike, licking his lips. Then he looked around to see which direction to head.

Mike explored several dig sites. There were scientists at each site, digging or sifting through small fragments of bone.

"Borrring!" Mike said, faking a yawn.

Just then, a flash of color caught the corner of his eye. A red-haired girl stood at the edge of a nearby forest. He watched as she slipped into the trees and away from the dig site.

Where's she going? wondered Mike. He ran toward a tall tree and started to climb for a better view.

Fwip! Fwip! Two sets of shiny white hooks burst from the cuffs of his Dino Jacket. They dug into the tree bark.

"Velociraptor claws!"
Mike exclaimed.

With help from the
claws, Mike quickly
reached the top of the
tree. He looked out over
the forest but didn't see
the mysterious girl.

Then Mike's eyes
suddenly grew wide.
On the forest floor, he
spotted what looked
like a large, slimy lizard
tail. It quickly slithered
out of view.

"A dinosaur tail!!" shouted Mike.

He scrambled out of the tree and started running back to the dig site. After a moment, he realized that what he saw couldn't possibly be a dinosaur.

Seconds later, a figure appeared in front of him. "Whoa!" Mike screamed, sliding to a stop on the muddy forest floor.

Mike looked up. Standing in front of him was the mysterious redhead.

"Why are you following me?" the girl asked, pointing a finger at him.

"I w-wasn't really," Mike stammered as he stood. "I was just w-wondering where you were going."

"It's not any of your business," the girl said, "but I was tracking something."

"The *dinosaur*?" Mike joked.

"You saw it?!" the girl shouted. Where did it go?" She pulled out a small, high-tech device. It was about the size of a cell phone. Mike couldn't figure out what the screen was displaying.

BOOOM! BOOOOM!

"Did you hear that?" she asked Mike.

"No, I didn't hear anything —"

BOOOM! BOOOOM!

The girl cut off Mike before he could finish his sentence. "There it is again!" The girl looked down at the ground and blurted out, "Uh-oh."

Mike followed her eyes to look down at what she had spotted. He wondered why she would be looking at a muddy puddle until he noticed ripples on the surface of the water. The ripples were happening faster and faster. Something was getting closer and closer.

"We need to run," said the girl as she started to back away from the puddle.

"Why?" asked Mike.

Answering his question, a giant T. rex charged out of the forest toward them.

ROOOAAR!

Chapter 3
RUN!

"Keep running!" the girl shouted.

Mike tried keeping up with her. He could feel the steamy breath of the real-life Tyrannosaurus rex chasing them.

Between gulps of air, Mike managed to say, "How . . . is this . . . possible?"

"Long story," said the girl, ducking under a tree branch. "But, yes, he's the real deal!"

Mike glanced behind him. "That can't possibly be a *real* dinosaur!" he said, trying to convince himself.

The girl suddenly turned left. Mike followed. The T. rex trailed the redhead like she had a target on her back.

"Your hair!" Mike exclaimed.

"What about it?" replied the girl between breaths.

"The T. rex," explained Mike, "he's following the color!"

"Oh my gosh!" said the girl. "My hood. I forgot!"

The girl quickly pulled her jacket hood over her bright red hair and then dove behind a tree. Mike did the same.

Beneath the cover of leaves, the duo kept as quiet as possible.

BOOOM! BOOOOM! The giant lizard stomped past them. Soon, his footsteps faded into the distance.

"You okay? Good," said the girl, not waiting for Mike's reply. "The best thing you can do is get out of here before that beast comes back."

The girl got up and looked around. Then she walked in the direction the T. rex was headed.

"Wait!" Mike called after her. "Where are you going?"

"I have work to do," she replied.

"B-but," Mike stuttered, "w-what w-was that thing?"

The girl continued walking away. "If you don't know what a dinosaur is," she said, "I don't have time to explain."

"I know what a dinosaur is. That was a tyrant lizard king!" Mike shouted. He used the meaning of the T. rex's scientific name to prove how much he knew about dinosaurs. "But they went extinct more than 65 million years ago!"

"I'm not surprised that you know so much," said the girl. "You're Mike Evans, right?"

"How did you know that?" he asked.

"Your father is one of the leading paleontologists in the country," she replied. "I was thinking about asking him for help, but he's — how do I put this nicely? — an adult."

The girl stopped. "You seem to know a lot about dinosaurs yourself," she told Mike. "How much do you *really* know?"

"Try me," he said.

"Okay." The girl smirked. "What's the spiky tail of a stegosaurus called?"

"A thagomizer," Mike quickly replied. "Now answer *me* a question. Let's pretend all of this is true. Let's pretend it's a real dinosaur, and you're going out there to look for it. What will you do when you find it?"

"Ha! That's a silly question, Mike," she said. "I'm gonna blast that dino back to the past!"

Chapter 4

MYSTERY GIRL

Mike followed the girl back to her campsite. When they got there, he stepped inside of the girl's small tent.

"'Whoa!" he exclaimed. The inside of the tent was filled with high-tech gadgets and equipment. Dozens of lights, buttons, and switches glowed all around.

"Who are you?" asked Mike, puzzled.

"I'm lots of things," said the girl. "But today, I'm a T. rex tracker."

"Tyrannosaurs are extinct!" Mike insisted. "They don't exist anymore."

"You still don't think it was real?" asked the girl. "You saw it with your own eyes. What else could it have been?"

"A Sasquatch?" suggested Mike.

"You're joking, right?" she said.

"Well, whatever that creature is," he began, ignoring her question, "how are you going to send it back to the past?"

The girl held a fancy device that Mike didn't recognize. "We are going to *track* him with this!"

Then the girl held up another device with her other hand. "And then we'll *catch* him with this," she explained.

Mike stared blankly at her.

"Come on," said the girl. "When will you ever have another chance to catch a real-life dinosaur?"

Mike couldn't help but smile at the thought. "That would be pretty cool," he told the mysterious girl.

"Good," she said, walking toward the exit of the tent. "Now, come on, let's go get that dino!"

"Wait," Mike called after her. "I don't even know your name."

The girl shuffled and fumbled the equipment in her arms in order to free a hand. She stuck it out toward Mike. "My name is Shannon," she said.

"Nice to meet you, Shannon," Mike replied, shaking her hand firmly.

Chapter 5

DINO DINNER

Shannon turned on the high-tech scanner. "This little baby reports the location of any nearby creature larger than an elephant," she said. "You don't have elephants in Montana, do you?"

"Nope," replied Mike.

Shannon pointed to a red dot on the scanner's screen. "Then *that's* our dino!"

"Really?!" Mike exclaimed.

"Yep," answered Shannon, "and he's heading toward the main dig site. I'd guess he's looking for food."

Mike took off running. "We have to stop that T. rex," he shouted, "before it eats anyone!"

Shannon ran to keep up with Mike. "T. rex are more scavengers than hunters, you know?" she explained.

"I know," Mike replied. "But I can't risk my dad becoming dino dinner!"

"How do you plan to stop him?" asked Shannon.

Mike stopped. "You said yourself that tyrannosaurs are scavengers, but how do they find their food?"

Shannon thought for a second. "Their olfactory senses are actually quite tremendous."

POOR EYESIGHT!

AMAZING SENSE OF SMELL!

VERY SHARP TEETH!

"Exactly!" Mike exclaimed. "The
T. rex has a *monster* sense of smell."

Mike turned and started sprinting in
a new direction.

"Where are you going?" asked
Shannon. "The dig site is this way."

"Yes," said Mike, "but base camp is
over here."

Shannon didn't understand, but she
followed anyway. When they reached
base camp, they hid behind a group
of trees. The area was decked out with
picnic tables, rows of barbecue grills,
and everything else anyone would need
for an outdoor cookout.

A few people were hanging a giant banner that read *DINOSAUR BBQ*.

"Why are we here?" Shannon asked.

Mike pointed. "For that!"

"The hot dog cart?" Shannon wondered aloud. "You're hungry?"

Mike smiled at her and said, "No, but I'm guessing the T. rex is starving . . ."

Chapter 6

HOT-DOGGIN!

"Are you sure you know how to drive this thing?" Mike asked Shannon.

The all-terrain hot dog cart sped down the hillside at top speed.

"Not really," replied Shannon to Mike's terrified reaction to her driving. "It can't be that difficult. After all, it has a giant picture of a hot dog on it!"

A thought flashed into Mike's brain.
The last time he went to an amusement
park, Mike's dad told him to keep his
arms and legs inside the ride. He was
thankful for that advice every time
Shannon narrowly missed a tree.

"How about you let me drive?" Mike
asked Shannon.

44

Shannon glanced at him and joked, "You don't look old enough to drive."

While technically true, Mike didn't think he had enough time to explain the entire summer of go-cart racing he'd done with his friends.

"Well, could you at least slow down?" said Mike, raising his voice.

He held on as they made another sharp turn to avoid an oak tree and took a hard bounce that nearly turned him around in his seat. The back hatch opened on the cart. Mike could see the hot dogs bouncing around inside. Some started spilling out.

Mike reached back and closed the lid. He needed every last hot dog for his big plan (which might not even work!).

As he reached back for the hot dogs, his hand felt different, as if there was a sudden change in temperature. Warmer and more humid — wait! Someone was breathing on his hand. Mike's eyes moved from his hand upward. Not someone. SomeTHING. Something big was breathing on his hand!

"Go," Mike muttered. "Go faster!"

Shannon huffed. "Seriously? Make up your mind! Do you want me to slow down or go faster?"

Mike moved as far to the front of the cart and away from the T. rex as possible. "Definitely go faster."

"ROOOAAR!"

Shannon didn't have to turn around to know what was directly behind her.

If the piercing roar wasn't a big enough clue, the blast of hot air from the dinosaur's breath that whipped her hair was a dead giveaway.

"We're almost at the dig site!" Mike shouted. "Only one way to see if Mr. Dino's olfactory system is working — give him a good whiff of hot dogs."

"Yes! Do it!" yelled Shannon as the T. rex loomed closer.

Mike picked up a fistful of hot dogs and threw his best fastball. The **SNAP** of the giant T. rex jaws grabbing hot dogs out of the air told him he had pretty good aim for his first pitch.

"We got his attention. Let's see if we can keep it!" said Shannon. She steered the golf cart away from the dig sites.

Mike threw a few more handfuls of hot dogs into the air.

"It's working!" he exclaimed as the dinosaur made the wide turn to follow them. "Although I'm not too sure why I'm so excited that we just got a huge T. rex to follow us!"

"You're excited because you're about to catch your first dino," said Shannon.

Mike didn't know if he should agree with her about that.

"Get ready to jump!" Shannon yelled.

"What —?!" Mike exclaimed. But the only response he got was the sight of Shannon leaping off the cart.

Not waiting to be told another time, Mike jumped off to the side just in time to see the T. rex jaws clamp down on the back end of the hot dog cart. **CRUNCH!**

Mike hit the ground hard and rolled to a stop. Behind him, he watched the dino rip apart the cart like an eggshell. Within seconds, the beast had eaten nearly every last hot dog.

"Shannon!" Mike said, scrambling to his feet.

Shannon was already busy preparing her equipment. Mike hesitated at first, not wanting to bother her, but then asked, "What do we do now?"

Without looking up, she replied, "Now that we've got him right where we want him —"

"This is where we want him?" Mike interrupted. "In the middle of the forest eating hot dogs?" He gestured toward the dinosaur. "Which, by the way, he's almost finished with, and I think he might still be hungry."

"Right. So hopefully he'll come after us next." Shannon smiled.

Mike started to agree with her.
"Yeah, hopefully — huh?!"

Just then, the T. rex gobbled up
the last of the hot dogs and turned
to them.

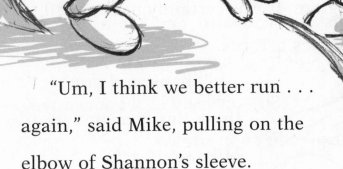

"Um, I think we better run . . .
again," said Mike, pulling on the
elbow of Shannon's sleeve.

Instead, Shannon moved forward toward the oncoming T. rex. She flipped open one of her gadgets and slid it on the ground toward the giant lizard.

Fwoosh! A blue laser-light beam burst from the gadget and formed a cube even bigger than the dinosaur.

Mike was confused. The blue cube was empty. He could see the outline that made up the edges of the cube, but it looked like nothing more than a hologram. It was certainly not enough to hold back a T. rex.

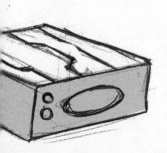

"Shannon, I don't think this is a good idea," Mike said.

Mike closed his eyes so he didn't have to see what he thought would happen next. A split second later, he opened one eye to peek anyway.

The T. rex entered the blue cube, and to Mike's surprise the beast was suddenly frozen in place. Things went quiet. The pounding footsteps no longer thundered. The heavy breathing of the massive creature stopped. The forest became peaceful once again.

Now Mike opened both eyes. He looked up to see the T. rex totally hypnotized. Mike marveled at just how big, strong, and dangerous it appeared.

"Wow." It was the only thing Mike could say. Then he followed up with, "How did you do that?"

"We call it a Trap-o-saur," Shannon said. "The safest way to capture dinos."

"He's . . . he's not in any pain, is he?" Mike asked, worried.

"No," Shannon explained. "I would never hurt a living creature. The trap puts the dinosaurs that enter its field into a sort of suspended animation. It's kind of like they're sleeping but actually awake at same time."

"Is it permanent?" asked Mike.

"No," she said. "He'll stay this way until we can come back and pick him up." She started gathering her other equipment. "Once we get him back where he belongs, he'll be released from the trap and be as good as new."

"Now that the danger is over," said Mike, "I'm kind of going to miss having a dinosaur running around here. Except for him wanting to eat us, of course!"

Shannon and Mike started to walk away from the dinosaur. "Mike," Shannon began, "you've been a big help. I don't know how to say thank you."

Mike chuckled. "Any time you need someone to help you chase down a dinosaur," he said, "call me."

Then, a **CRUNCH** echoed through the forest behind them. Shannon and Mike both froze in their tracks.

"Did you just hear that?" asked Mike.

Mike turned around slowly.

"It sounded exactly like —" Shannon began.

CRUNCH came the sound again from behind them.

"— The footsteps of a dinosaur!" Mike finished her thought.

Mike and Shannon looked at each other, not wanting to turn around. When they did, the duo spotted their old friend: T. rex! The oversized beast had broken out of his trap.

CRUNCH! CRASH! He stomped toward them, even angrier than before.

"H-how did he get free?" said Mike.

"I don't know," answered Shannon. "The only way he could have gotten out of the Trap-o-saur would be if —"

"Someone set him free?" came a nearby voice.

A shadowy figure stepped out from behind a tree.

The stranger was holding a small object. It looked like the same type of technology Shannon had used. The device had a red laser-like blade that was obviously just used to cut the blue laser cube holding the T. rex in place.

"Let me guess," said Shannon, "*you* set the T. rex free?"

Mike was surprised by this stranger but noticed that Shannon was not.

"I thought you might still be here," Shannon added.

"Of course," said the stranger. "I had to make sure the T. rex I brought here got the chance to stay here."

As the T. rex stepped closer to Shannon and Mike, the mysterious figure stepped out of the shadows. He was a tall boy, older than Mike and Shannon by a year or two.

He was dressed in a purple shirt and black pants. Mike could barely see the stranger's eyes as his hair almost covered them completely.

Mike was about to ask the person who he was when he heard Shannon mutter a name . . .

"Jurassic Jeff."

Chapter 7

JURASSIC JEFF

"Who?" asked Mike.

"Jeff," answered the stranger. "That's me. I'm the one and only Jurassic Jeff."

Mike said, "Your mom actually named you Jurassic Jeff?"

CRUNCH! SMASH! CRUNCH!

Just then, the T. rex advanced slowly toward Mike and Shannon.

The stranger smiled. "I think you've got more important things to worry about at the moment," he said, "like a giant T. rex coming straight for you!"

"Jeff," Shannon pleaded.

The T. rex stomped a clawed foot toward them. **Whump!** Shannon started to back away. "I know I've said this before but . . . RUN!" she screamed.

"You don't have to tell me twice," Mike responded, following closely behind her.

The T. rex gave chase. They could hear Jurassic Jeff call out, "Be seeing you around Shannon . . . *maybe*."

The duo ran under fallen logs, between tight spaces, and over rocks. The T. rex easily crossed, crushed, barreled through each obstacle.

"He's not stopping!" huffed Mike.

The duo came to a stop in an area surrounded by tall trees. With the T. rex behind them, they turned and backed up until they were against a large boulder. They were both too tired to go on.

Nearly out of breath, Shannon said, "I can't . . . run . . . anymore."

The T. rex slowed down and closed in, sensing that his prey was now cornered.

"I don't think it matters anyway. We're trapped," replied Mike.

The T. rex eyed them closely. The beast leaned down and gave the duo a long hard sniff.

"I'm so sorry I got you involved," said Shannon. She reached over and squeezed Mike's forearm tightly.

ROOOOOOOAAAARRR!!

The sudden noise startled everyone, especially the T. rex. The dinosaur stumbled around like a frightened animal. Leaves and branches scattered in every direction as the T. rex couldn't seem to get its footing.

Once it gained some balance, the T. rex turned and quickly ran away.

Amazed, Mike watched the entire scene play out in front of his eyes. They could hear the T. rex whimpering away into the forest.

"Uh, what happened?" asked Mike.

Shannon looked at him equally puzzled. "I don't know." She moved toward Mike. "I was scared, so I reached over and grabbed your arm . . ." She repeated the action once again, grabbing Mike's arm. "Like this."

"ROOOAARRR!!" A powerful growl erupted from Mike's Dino Jacket.

It was the same loud, rumbling roar that startled them and sent the T. rex running off like a scared rabbit.

"Your hoodie!" exclaimed Shannon.

"It roars!" finished Mike. "Sorry, I didn't know it could do that."

"You're apologizing?" asked Shannon.

"For a second, I thought it was my video game," said Mike. "That thing goes off on its own sometimes."

Shannon hugged Mike tighter than he had ever been hugged before. "You saved us!" she exclaimed.

Mike turned a bright shade of red. "I didn't mean to, but I guess I did." Mike smiled. "I guess that's one of the cool surprises my dad put in this jacket."

"Well, be sure to tell him I said thank you!" said Shannon. "You know, that T. rex hasn't heard any other dinosaurs since it's been here. We're lucky your roar startled it. It could have easily been attracted to the sound."

Mike brushed the leaves off his jacket. "So who was that guy back there?" he asked.

"Jurassic Jeff. And he's nothing but a troublemaker," Shannon explained.

"Jeff is from where I'm from," Shannon continued. "He thinks dinos should never have gone extinct. He's trying to save them by introducing them into different time periods. Unfortunately, he doesn't realize how much damage he's doing or how many people he's putting in danger. That's why I've come back here to stop him, and we were so close. We had the T. rex captured! Jeff must have known I was here and was following me."

"Let's get this straight," began Mike. "You came back here to capture a T. rex and bring him back to his own time."

"Yep." Shannon nodded.

"Because it was taken by a crazy guy who likes to call himself Jurassic Jeff?" Mike finished.

"Sounds strange, right?" she said.

Mike let out a long breath. "If I hadn't just almost been eaten by a T. rex, I don't think I would have believed one word of your story." He was silent for a moment and then asked, "So what do we do now?"

"I can't ask for any more help than you've already given," said Shannon.

"Are you kidding?" said Mike. "I always finish what I've started."

"Besides," Mike continued, "now you've got Jurassic Jeff out there looking to undo anything you do. I'm helping! I love dinosaurs too. It was cool to actually see one, but even I know it doesn't belong here."

"That's nice of you to say," said Shannon. "I knew when I saw you that I could trust you."

"Do you have more of those Trap-o-saur things?" asked Mike.

"Yes." Shannon nodded.

"Then what are we waiting for?" said Mike. "Let's go get Sam!"

"Sam?" asked Shannon, confused.

Mike answered, "The T. rex."

"You named the T. rex?" she asked again, still confused.

"We've been chased by him twice now. I feel like we've gotten to know him," Mike explained.

Mike continued, "It felt weird to keep calling him the T. rex or the Dinosaur, so I figured I'd give him a name . . . you know, temporarily."

"Sam . . ." said Shannon. "I like it."

Chapter 8

BIG PROBLEMS

A short time later, the duo was almost at Shannon's campsite when Mike confessed. "I still can't believe that guy calls himself Jurassic Jeff."

"There's nothing wrong with having a nickname," said Shannon.

"Oh yeah?" said Mike. "What should I call you . . . Silly Shannon?"

"If you must make something up for me, you could be nicer," said Shannon. "I already have a nickname. My brother used to call me Triceratops Shannon."

Mike laughed. "Really? Triceratops Shannon?"

"There's a reason," she said, "but I don't know if I want to tell you now."

"Oh, come on!" encouraged Mike. "You have to now. You can't leave me with a name like Triceratops Shannon and not expect me to be curious."

As they crunched through the leaves, it was obvious that Shannon was a bit embarrassed.

"When I was little I would wear my hair in a silly way," Shannon explained. "I would straighten and tease my hair so that it would stick up in the front and on the sides. It would look like I had three horns sticking out of my head that would make me look like —"

Mike guessed and tried to finish her sentence. "A Triceratops?"

"Yep, the three-horned dinosaur," confirmed Shannon.

"Hmm . . ." Mike rubbed his chin, puzzled. "I don't see the resemblance."

Shannon pulled her hair into spikes, and Mike let out a laugh.

Mike didn't stop laughing until they reached the campsite. It was in ruins. The tent was knocked over, and nearly everything was broken.

The look on Shannon's face told Mike that she was not surprised to see the campsite destroyed.

"What happened?" asked Mike.

Shannon just blurted out, "Jeff." She walked through the wreckage, picking up anything she could salvage. "He did this to make sure I wouldn't have any equipment to catch the T. rex."

"But all of your stuff," said Mike. "What are we going to do?"

Shannon looked at Mike. "When you've had a few run-ins with Jurassic Jeff, you learn to be prepared," she said.

Shannon picked up a small camping shovel and walked over to her broken tent. She flipped over the tent and started to dig underneath.

"What are you doing?" asked Mike.

"Digging out the extra equipment I hid," she said. "I knew Jeff might do something like this."

Mike smiled. "So you let Jeff destroy your stuff, but you have more stuff?"

"Yep," she answered. "Hidden down here, buried under my tent."

"You're pretty smart," said Mike, complimenting her.

Shannon smiled. "Thanks. They don't call me Triceratops Shannon for nothing." She unearthed a box and pulled it up from the hole. "Triceratops are smarter than most people think."

Shannon gathered all of the equipment from the box. She handed some to Mike.

"Now we need to find out where Sam went before people discover there's a real dinosaur on the loose," she said.

Mike decided to be bolder with his questions. After all, they had been through quite a bit together. "So you come from a different time, don't you?"

Shannon looked nervous for a moment. Then she said, "I really appreciate all the help you've given. I've never met someone as nice and as helpful as you."

After a pause, Shannon said, "But I think the less you know about all of this stuff — who I am or where that dinosaur came from — the better."

"But —" Mike began.

Before he could say more, she continued. "I know it's not fair to you. If it were up to me, I would give you all the answers to your questions, but you're just going to have to trust me."

"Okay," said Mike. "If that's the way you want it."

A split second later, Shannon dove at Mike, tackling him in a giant bear hug.

Shannon realized she was squeezing Mike really hard and let him go. Her face turned red as they exchanged no words in the awkward moment.

"So . . ." Mike said, breaking the silence, "are we going to look for Sam or what?"

Chapter 9
TROUBLE

Mike stood in the middle of an open area surrounded by trees. He was thinking about one of the last things Shannon said to him: "The real question is, where's Jurassic Jeff?"

She warned him that he could be anywhere and could surprise them at any time.

Mike reached over with his right hand and squeezed his left arm. The Dino Jacket let out a loud roar.

ROOOOAAAAR!

He had gotten used to the sound by now. He was also making sure not to repeat it too many times. He squeezed the jacket again.

ROOOOAAAAR!

Mike looked around to make sure he didn't see any red hair.

Nope. Good.

That meant Shannon had her hoodie on, hiding her hair. He knew she was hidden somewhere around the area.

If he could not see her, Jurassic Jeff couldn't see her either.

"What are you doing out here?" came a voice from behind one of the surrounding trees.

"Give it up, Jeff," shouted Mike. "Even though you screwed up her last capture attempt, we finally got the T. rex, and she left with it."

"That's impossible!" Jeff screamed. He stepped out from behind the trees. "I've been tracking it. It was heading in this direction, and I also heard it roar."

"Oh, you mean *this* roar?" Mike said, squeezing the arm of his jacket again.

ROOOOAAAAR!

"How did you —?" said Jeff.

"From what I understand," said Mike, interrupting, "the sound should attract the T. rex here, making him think there are other dinosaurs."

As if on cue, the now-familiar sound of stomping and leaf crushing was growing louder from the distance.

CRUNCH! SMASH! BOOM!

The T. rex Mike had nicknamed Sam burst through the thick foliage of the trees and into the open area. Mike could tell by the look on Jeff's face that he was surprised again.

As Sam raced forward, Mike did not want to miss his chance. He threw down a trap. It quickly unfolded into a blue see-through cube. Before Sam could realize what was happening, the dinosaur was trapped inside.

"HEY!" yelled Jeff. "That's my dinosaur!"

The boy started running toward Mike with what Mike could only assume was the same laser-knife he had used to cut Sam free from the last trap.

"I thought you said Shannon already left with it!" screamed Jeff.

"We tricked you!" said Shannon.

She came running from the tree line, pulling off her hoodie to reveal her red hair so that Jeff would recognize that it was her. As she got closer, she threw down another trap. This one landed directly in front of Jeff's path.

The big blue cubed erected itself just as Jeff stepped into it. Jurassic Jeff was now as motionless as the T. rex.

"Wow!" I can't believe that worked," said Shannon, sighing a deep breath of relief. "I contacted my team, and they should be at my campsite any minute."

"What are you waiting for?" said Mike. "Let's get going!"

Shannon gave Mike one last hug and said, "Thanks for everything."

Mike looked over at Jeff and saw he had activated the laser cutter he was holding in his hand. He was cutting his way free.

"GO!" yelled Mike as he pushed Shannon toward the T. rex.

Shannon put her hands on the blue cube and pushed it toward the forest.

Mike had never seen anything like it. A large blue-edged cube with a life-size T. rex inside of it rolled through the forest, hovering about two inches above the ground.

As Shannon effortlessly pushed the cube along, Mike followed right behind her. He was sure that Jurassic Jeff was not far behind him.

"Get to the campsite!" said Mike.

"What about you?" asked Shannon.

"Don't worry about me," replied Mike. "You get out of here and get Sam back where he belongs. I'll distract Jeff."

Shannon continued to roll the giant caged T. rex through the forest. Mike heard her say, "Thank you . . ." But he couldn't make out the rest of what she said as she disappeared.

Without wasting any time, Mike pulled together a large pile of leaves around him. He disappeared down into the leaves.

All was quiet for a few seconds until he could hear the trampling of sticks and leaves. It was Jeff, hot on their trail.

Mike waited until Jeff was almost on top of him, and then he surprised him. Mike burst out of the leaves, pulling his hoodie up over his head.

Beep! Beep! The T. rex eyes on Mike's hoodie activated. The blinding light shined right at Jeff's face.

"Ahhhhh!! My eyes!" screamed Jeff. "I can't see!" He rubbed his eyes, trying to regain his vision.

Mike used the opportunity to run and catch up with Shannon.

"You may have blinded me with those bright lights for a few seconds, but I can still hear you!" shouted Jeff.

He's right! thought Mike. *If he can hear my footsteps and I try to follow Shannon, he'll catch us and have the T. rex again.*

Jeff was bleary-eyed but could finally see again. "My vision is back!" he exclaimed. "Now I'll find you —"

But he did not see anyone as he looked around. "Hey! Where did you go?" Jeff shouted.

Jeff looked behind one tree and then another. He looked behind all the trees in the area but did not see anyone.

"You're just wasting time, kid. I'll find you . . ." He stopped. "Oh no. That's what you wanted. You wanted me to follow you so I wouldn't follow her. You tricked me into looking for you so I would waste time."

Jeff realized that the minutes he spent looking for Mike gave Shannon enough time to get away.

"Curse you!" said Jeff, shaking his hand in the air. "You've been nothing but trouble, kid!"

Jeff stomped off. "You better hope we never meet again!" he mumbled and grumbled his way through the forest.

Mike could hear less and less of Jeff's complaints the farther away he got. The reason Jeff couldn't find him hiding behind any tree was because he wasn't behind a tree . . .

He was *up* in a tree!

Mike had not gone more than five feet from the pile of leaves.

He realized Jeff was right.

He had temporarily blinded Jeff, but Mike could still hear what direction he was going in. Mike used his retractable dinosaur claws and climbed instead.

Lucky for him, Jeff never thought to look up.

Chapter 10
DINO EGGS!

Mike made his way to Shannon's campsite. There was no sign of her ever having been there except for the spot they dug to find her hidden equipment. Even the dirt was smoothed over.

Shannon's departure must have went as planned, and thanks to him she was able to get there with Sam the T. rex.

Mike thought about the day's adventure as he made his way through the forest to the dig site where his father was located. He probably didn't have to worry about Jurassic Jeff anymore either. With Shannon and Sam the T. rex gone, Jeff was probably gone too.

He was not going to miss that guy or the big scary dinosaur . . . but his other friend, Triceratops Shannon, was a different story. He would miss her.

As he came to the dig site, he could see it was getting close to sundown. The science teams were packing up their equipment for the night.

Mike noticed the large tree on the other side of the dig site. That was the tree he decided to climb when he first spotted the mysterious stranger, Shannon. Even though he knew her now, he still decided she was a mysterious stranger because he didn't know much about her or where she was from.

Mike smiled though because that was the same tree that changed his life. That's when he first spotted Sam the T. rex.

Mike turned around to look at the forest. He was standing not far from the spot where he first saw the tail of that giant lizard. Just a few feet away behind those trees was where the T. rex, from a time long past, was stomping around just a few short hours ago.

He walked over to the edge of the dig site and saw all the flags and posts marking where bones were buried. He could see people working to dig up the bones of something he saw walking around just a little while ago. It was hard to believe that millions of years later this is how dinos would end up.

He looked down and saw a large grassy area. As his eyes swept the spot, something white caught his attention. He thought they were just rocks piled in the grass. That was strange, but the way they were clumped together looked out of sorts.

Mike decided to take a closer look. For a second, he thought it was weird that the rocks looked more like giant eggs than they did rocks. He was about to reach down and pick one up when he suddenly heard a familiar voice.

"Mike?" Mike turned to see his dad coming toward him. He was walking along the edge of the dig site. Mike was easy to spot in the middle of the open area of the grass between the edge of the dig site and the forest.

"I've been looking for you everywhere, son. The big barbecue is about to start. You must be hungry."

"Yeah, I am!" replied Mike, realizing that he hadn't eaten all day.

"Hey, what have you got there?" asked his dad as he got closer.

Mike looked down at the odd-shaped rocks at his feet.

"I'm not sure," said Mike, "but I think they're eggs."

Mike could see his dad's eyes grow almost twice as big as normal.

"Dad? What's the matter?" said Mike.

"Son!" exclaimed his dad. "You just found dinosaur eggs!"

"What?!" cried Mike.

His dad took a closer look. "These are so well preserved too! I've never seen anything like this!"

He yelled down to the team that was packing up equipment on the dig site. "Hey! We've got something over here! Bring up some lights and equipment as fast as you can!"

Dad turned to Mike and held him excitedly by the shoulders. "This is incredible! The first day I ever bring you to a dinosaur dig, and you've made one of the biggest finds ever!"

Just then, beeping sounds started coming from Mike's pocket.

Dad laughed and patted Mike on the back. "Don't you ever turn that video game off?" He turned to give his team instructions on how to proceed. Then he ended by telling Mike, "Museums all over the world are going to go crazy!"

Mike smiled. After the day he had had he couldn't think it would get any better, but now this?

It was crazy! The video game in his pocket beeped loud sounds again.

Thinking that he had forgot to turn it off, Mike pulled it out of his pocket.

The screen read, "Hello, Mike!"

That was strange. He pressed the buttons, and the message scrolled. It read: "Hope you don't mind, but I found your game frequency. I figured I would send you a message telling you how thankful I am for your help! Also how unfair it was that you had to deal with Jurassic Jeff and that you found out my nickname was Triceratops (LOL). Anyway, I have decided that you need a nickname too! So thanks again for all your help . . . DINO-MIKE!"

Mike scrolled down to the bottom of the message.

"P.S.: Sam the T. rex made the trip home in great condition. FYI: Sam is actually Samantha! How funny is that?"

Mike laughed to himself at what he just read. Then, something suddenly occurred to him.

Mike's face went blank as he watched his dad and his team lift the eggs and place them into a padded box.

He thought, *Sam is actually a . . . GIRL!!*

Sam the T. rex wasn't coming to the dig site to look for food. Samantha the T. rex was coming to the dig site to look for her eggs!

As the crate was sealed shut, Mike whispered, "Uh-oh."

Time for another adventure! thought Dino-Mike.

GLOSSARY

extinct (ek-STINGKT)—something that no longer exists; dinosaurs are extinct, so they no longer exist

fossil (FOSS-uhl)—the remains or traces of an animal or plant from millions of years ago, preserved in rock

Jurassic Period (juh-RA-sik PIHR-ee-uhd)—a period of time about 200 to 144 million years ago

paleontologist (pale-ee-uhn-TOL-uh-gist)—a scientist that deals with fossils and other life-forms

triceratops (try-SER-uh-tops)—a large, plant-eating dinosaur with three horns and a fan-shaped collar of bone

tyrannosaurus (ti-RAN-uh-sor-uhs)—a large, meat-eating dinosaur that walked on its hind legs, also known as a T. rex

DINO FACTS!

Did you know the scientific name Tyrannosaurus rex (ti-RAN-uh-sor-uhs REX) means "Tyrant Lizard King"? Weighing 5 to 7 tons, this dino really was reptile royalty.

The T. rex was the star of the movie *Jurassic Park*, but these dinos didn't live during the Jurassic Period. They lived between 65 to 85 million years ago during a time known as the Cretaceous period (kri-TAY-shush PIHR-ee-uhd).

At 40 feet long and 20 feet tall, the T. rex was one of the largest meat-eating dinos ever.

Scientists believe T. rex could chase down prey at more than 40 miles per hour.

The T. rex's arms were surprisingly small. At only 3 feet long, they were too short to capture prey. Instead of grabbing prey with its tiny arms, T. rex grabbed food with its teeth. Each T. rex tooth measured more than 9 inches long!

T. rex used its giant teeth to satisfy a giant appetite. With one bite, scientists believe the T. rex could gobble up about 500 pounds of meat.

All of the T. rex fossils discovered have been found in North America. In 1990, one of the best-known and most complete skeletons was discovered in South Dakota by fossil hunter Sue Hendrickson. The fossil, known simply as "Sue," is now on display at the Field Museum in Chicago.

ABOUT THE AUTHOR

Bronx, New York-born writer and artist Franco Aureliani has been drawing comics since he could hold a crayon. Currently residing in upstate New York with his wife, Ivette, and son, Nicolas, he spends most of his days in his Batcave-like studio where he works on comics projects. In 1995, Franco founded Blindwolf Studios, an independent art studio where he and fellow creators can create children's comics. Franco is the creator, artist, and writer of Weirdsville, L'il Creeps, and Eagle All Star, as well as the cocreator and writer of Patrick the Wolf Boy.

Franco recently finished work on Superman Family Adventures and is now cowriting the series The Green Team: Teen Trillionaires and Tiny Titans by DC Comics. When he's not writing and drawing, Franco teaches high school art.